Dick Whittington

For my children, Thea and Freddie

First published 2012 by A & C Black,
an imprint of Bloomsbury Publishing Plc
50 Bedford Square
London WC1B 3DP

www.bloomsbury.com

Copyright © 2012 A & C Black
Text copyright © 2012 Clare Gifford
Illustrations copyright © 2012 Emmanuel Cerisier

HB ISBN 978-1-4081-8761-6
PB ISBN 978-1-4081-8762-3

A CIP catalogue for this book is available from the British Library.

This book is produced using paper that is made from wood
grown in managed, sustainable forests. It is natural, renewable and
recyclable. The logging and manufacturing processes conform
to the environmental regulations of the country of origin.

1 3 5 7 9 10 8 6 4 2

Printed in China by C&C Offset Printing Co., Ltd., Shenzhen, Guandong

Dick Whittington

Clare Gifford
Illustrated by Emmanuel Cerisier

A & C BLACK
AN IMPRINT OF BLOOMSBURY
LONDON NEW DELHI NEW YORK SYDNEY

No one has ever become poor by giving.
Anne Frank (1929–1945)

ick blew on his numb fingers and tried again to grip the last turnip and pull it from the frozen ground. He carried the heavy basket inside to where his mother nursed his newest little sister, while his two big brothers were scrapping and squabbling over the last hunk of a loaf. Dick cleaned the vegetables, stoked the fire, tidied the parlour and fed Tom the cat. Then he went to the room that he shared with his brothers and sisters, lit a candle and settled once more to learning his letters.

One day, when watery sunlight dappled through the trees, and the snow had almost thawed, Dick saw little green shoots nosing their way through the black earth.

'Mother,' he said, 'it is hard for you in this little house, with Father away, and so many of us to look after. Soon I shall be old enough to go to London and seek my fortune. When I come back, all our hardship will be just a memory.'

It was hard to leave, knowing that his mother would have less help without him, so it wasn't until the autumn that Dick set off from his little village of Pauntley. He had never been beyond the great forest before, and he was excited and just a little frightened by the prospect of his journey.

Hungry, tired and footsore, he arrived on the second day in the city of Gloucester. He earned some pennies by helping the masons who were building a great cathedral there. He bought some soft leather boots with good strong soles and set off again, full of excitement in the warm sunshine.

On the road near Burford he saw a tired young woman struggling with her small children and burdened with the produce that she was taking to market.

Dick wondered how his mother would be coping back at home, working so hard to look after his brothers and sisters, and he forgot his excitement as his eyes pricked with tears. He helped the woman carry her vegetables to the market square and continued towards Oxford with a heavy heart, wondering if he was doing the right thing.

Oxford! The magnificent bustling city filled him with hope and joy once again.

As he walked beside the walled garden of St Frideswide's, a canon emerged and placed a small dish of milk on the doorstep for a large grey cat which was winding herself around his cassock.

'Good Puss,' Dick heard the man say, 'so many mice! What are we to do?'

Dick called, 'Good evening, Father,' and was met with a weary smile.

'Young man, it is indeed a fine and beautiful evening as God's crimson orb bathes us in its blessed light. But here in the Priory the Good Lord has beset us with mice, and He has left us only old Puss, who does her best; but we are all at our wits' end!'

Dick helped the canons to move all the food in the pantry out of reach of the rodents, and then he helped them to scrub the floor and shelves.

'Perhaps,' Dick said, 'you might get yourself some young kittens to help your old puss?'

'Indeed, indeed, we will wait and the Lord will provide,' murmured the canon.

Dick spent a comfortable night in the Priory. Fortified with a breakfast of porridge and ale, he set off once again. The sun was rising, slanting its rays across the meadows, glinting on the river. In two days he would be in London, a city greater even than Oxford. Even its streets were paved with gold!

Dick walked night and day, such was his desire to be in London at last. In his exhausted imagination he saw the golden pavements, spires and domes in the magical city of his dreams. He saw men and women in gorgeous, sumptuous gowns, woven with silk and priceless metals; he saw carriages pulled by fine glistening horses with polished hooves; he even imagined he heard music and saw dancing!

After two days and nights with almost no rest or food, trudging between fields, Dick found himself in Watling Street. In the damp dawn mist, the tall stone walls of Newgate prison loomed above him, grey and forbidding.

As he crossed the River Fleet a horrible smell rose up from the dark water. Holding his nose, he looked down and saw rotting rubbish and excrement covering the muddy banks. The rutted road was fouled with every kind of waste, and his new boots started to leak as he stepped in oozing puddles.

He hesitated at the Greyfriars hospital where a ragged dirty crowd of thin, gaunt men, women and children were huddled at the gate. A grubby small girl, the same age as one of his sisters, begged for some money. He gave her one of his last pennies, thinking, 'Soon I shall be walking on the shining streets, between elegant buildings. I will find work, and be paid in gold! Then I shall help these poor people as well as my family.'

As the mist cleared he saw the pointed spire of St Paul's Cathedral, and his heart soared. But when he looked around, he saw the street around him was full of shuffling tired people, bent and weary, looking only at the ground, and he began to doubt the stories about London which had filled his head as a child.

Dick was tired and worn out. As he walked along Leadenhall Street he felt so exhausted and chilled through that he sheltered in a large doorway. He sat down and hunched in the corner, curling his body over his knees to protect himself from the rain, which was becoming heavier and heavier. For the first time he started to cry. The world seemed so big, so full of so many struggling people, and he felt small, cold and hungry.

* * *

Mr Fitzwarren, a wealthy cloth merchant, climbed down from his carriage and sighed. He had been to St Bartholomew's Hospital to visit one of his grooms and found that he had already died from typhus, leaving a wife and young children. He was wondering how best to help them and was lost in his thoughts when he noticed what looked like a pile of old clothes in his doorway.

'Um, er, hullo?' he said.

Dick lifted his head and saw a pair of legs in fine hose and beautiful leather shoes. 'Oh, sir, I am so sorry.' He scrambled to his feet, wiping his eyes on the back of his hand. 'I was just resting – I'll be away now.'

'Where will you go?' said the merchant gently.

'Somewhere… anywhere…' mumbled Dick, to the man's rotund tummy. He realised that he had no idea where to go in this huge, noisy, dirty city, and found his eyes filling with tears again.

He felt a warm, firm hand on his shoulder. When he looked up, the kindly face of Mr Fitzwarren was peering into his.

'Well, young man,' the merchant said, 'you don't sound much like a Londoner to me. Where have you come from?'

'From past Gloucester, sir. I walked here to find the golden pavements and take some money home for my poor mother – she works so hard and can hardly feed us all.'

'Poor you. This great city is as full of hardship as anywhere else. More so, I sometimes think. Are you tired? Hungry?'

'Yes, sir.'

'Are you willing to work for your board and lodging and three pennies a week?'

'Yes, sir!' answered Dick eagerly.

'What can you do?'

'I helped my mother in the garden, and I can prepare vegetables and keep the kitchen clean,' said Dick.

'Then you shall be a helper in my scullery. Come with me.'

Mr Fitzwarren's house was a hive of activity. There were many servants, all buzzing around like busy bees, and a constant stream of packages of rich textiles and fabrics were carried in and out of the yard. Wealthy ladies and gentlemen drew up at the front door in smart carriages and Dick loved to peek at their shining horses and beautiful garments.

He worked from before dawn until after sunset, and as the newest, most ignorant and youngest servant he was given all the worst jobs. The kitchen maids giggled and tittered every time he spoke and the footmen imitated his Gloucester accent. Worst of all, every week, Cook made him hand over his thruppence to pay for his food and bed. How would he ever save money for his family if he had to spend all his wages to live?

Every week the servants all lined up and Mr Fitzwarren gave them their pay. Dick waited at the end of the line for his thruppence. He looked forward to this because sometimes Mr Fitzwarren's daughter Alice came down to see them on payday. She was about his age and was the most beautiful thing he'd ever seen in his life. Sometimes she seemed almost to smile at him, but he thought that she was probably just trying not to laugh at him, like everyone else.

Occasionally when he was working, scrubbing the kitchen table, or peeling vegetables, or emptying rubbish, he would see her fleetingly from the corner of his eye. But as soon as he turned to smile, she was gone.

One day she stopped and spoke to him.

'Dick,' she said, 'what will you do with all the pennies and shillings that you are saving up?'

'I have none,' he said. 'I would have liked to send some to my mother, but Cook needs my money each week to pay for my food.'

Alice's eyes flashed and her pretty face flushed a delicate pink. She turned, pushed past the butler and ran back upstairs.

That afternoon Cook was summoned upstairs.

The next time Dick saw her, Cook spat on his shoes, and the following day she deliberately spilled greasy hot water all down his jerkin. But she never demanded his thruppence again.

At night Dick slept in a cellar under the pavement. It was chilly and damp, but the worst thing was that it was full of rats and mice, searching for a way into the kitchen. They gnawed holes in his clothes and made nests in his blankets, and at night they woke him by walking over his face or tugging his hair. And they smelt awful!

Once, after payday, Alice called him back. 'How are you, Dick?' she asked. 'I see you working so hard. I hope you are happy here, and not missing your country home too much.'

'I do miss my mother, and brothers and sisters,' he answered, 'but one day I shall be able to go back and help them again.

The thing I miss the most is my cat. I sleep so badly here because of all the rats in the cellar.'

'Oh! You poor thing!' Alice cried. 'I would hate to be without my Big Puss, although he's far too lazy to chase rats.'

A few days later, the sweep and his boy Jack came to the back door in the yard.

'Master Dick?' he asked.

'That's me!' said Dick.

'We just cleaned the chimneys upstairs and we heard lovely Alice talking to Mr Fitzwarren about cats and rats and what have you. We have cats – too many for my liking! Come over and take one. Yours for thruppence!'

So that was how Dick got his Tomkin, a big stripy tomcat with thick fur, white feet and black ears. In no time Dick's cellar was free of rats and mice, and Dick slept, warm and comfortable, with Tomkin curled against his chest.

A few days later, when Dick was in the yard giving Tomkin a dish of kitchen scraps, he heard a window open upstairs.

'Psst, Dick!' It was Alice, cuddling a huge orange cat. 'Look, this is Big Puss,' she said.

'And this is Tomkin,' he said, stroking his own cat. 'He's a great mouser and he keeps me warm too!'

Alice laughed, her eyes sparkling. 'I'm so glad,' she said, waved, and was gone.

One day Mr Fitzwarren called all his staff up to the salon for a special announcement. He was sending another ship to Barbary, laden with goods from the City of London, and it would bring back rich and exotic spices, textiles and gems. His last voyage to Barbary had been a great success, so this time he wanted to reward his staff. 'I would like each of you to send something of your own on my ship, the Unicorn, and with luck we will make good trade for you and bring you back a nice profit.'

There was great excitement as all the staff discussed what they would send: a trinket or garment, a belt or ring. Dick alone had nothing to send, and went back to the scullery feeling miserable.

That evening, as he was giving Tomkin his supper in the yard, Alice called to him from the window. 'Dick, really you should send something with Father. He will bring you money back, and you can help your family then.'

'But Miss Alice, I have nothing… except Tomkin!'

'Then you must send him! At least he will be useful chasing all the rats on board ship!'

So that was how Tomkin found himself aboard the Unicorn. Mr Fitzwarren specially asked the cabin boy to look after him, and Tomkin soon became a popular and very valuable crew member.

Time went by. Dick worked hard, but the rats came back to his cellar and spoiled his clothes. He spent his saved pennies on new ones. He lived for his glimpses of Alice and her radiant smile. Once, Big Puss came down to the kitchen and, since it was no place for such a well-bred animal, Dick carried him back up to Alice in the salon. Their eyes met, and their hands touched, as he gave the creature back.

Dick was thrilled, but the more he thought about the rich, lovely Alice, the more he realised how hopeless it all was. He had no money, no possessions, and no prospects. He was working for Fitzwarren's household when he could be helping his family in Gloucestershire. How pointless it all seemed. He decided to go home.

Dick set off past St Bartholomew's Hospital and through the Cripplegate. He was glad to leave behind the bustle and stench, the hard work and the beggars. But when he thought about leaving Alice, he felt as though his heart would break.

He headed uphill through woodlands and past lakes towards Highgate.

Meanwhile, the Unicorn had reached the Barbary Coast. Mr Fitzwarren's Captain and his men had been invited to the King of Barbary's palace, to bring their goods for trading. Excellent exchanges were made and the crew carried treasures from the mountain villages, the desert tribes and the coastal ports back to the ship.

Then everyone was invited to join the King for a banquet. The King and all his Queens appeared in splendid robes and finery and the Captain looked very dashing in his fine clothes.

As soon as they were seated and the feast dishes were brought in, there was a scuttling and a scuffling – then a swarm of rats poured in to the Banqueting Hall!

Through every door and window, from behind every pillar and curtain
and through every tiny crack; brown and black rats, yellow and white ones.
They fell on the food with excited squeaks and waving tails before the King
or any of his Queens or guests had managed a single bite.

'I apologise,' said the King to the Captain. 'This is our plague. Every day we try something new, but we cannot be rid of these vermin.'

'What you need is a cat,' said the Captain. 'That would fix them!'

'What is this thing you speak of: a cat?' asked the King.

'It is a soft, warm, flexible little beast, with sharp eyes, sharp teeth and sharp claws,' said the Captain. 'And it kills rats!'

'I must get myself a cat at any price!' exclaimed the King. 'But I have never seen such a creature. Where can I find one?'

'Well,' said the Captain carefully, 'we do just happen to have one on board the Unicorn. But Tomkin is a most valuable animal and protects all Mr Fitzwarren's belongings, and all our food, from the ravages of rats and mice. For the English cats are the best in Europe. And also, Tomkin is our friend.'

The King was amazed. 'This creature is a friend, as well as a killer? He is worth riches indeed! Bring me this Tomkin. I must see for myself if your cat can do as you say.'

Tomkin was feeling lonely and hungry on board the Unicorn as all the other crew members were ashore at the banquet. He was just settling down for a snooze on the deck when the cabin boy ran in.

'Come along, Tom, you're needed. Come and show everyone how brilliant you are!'

And when Tomkin saw all the rats in the great Banqueting Hall of the King of Barbary, he bounded from the boy's arms with elegant quickness, wreathing his body hither and thither as he leapt to catch the rats. Time after time he found his mark, with a mixture of gravity and waggery.

The King and his Queens and the whole court were astounded. When the rats were all killed or had fled, Tomkin sauntered over to the Number One Queen, sat down carefully beside her and proceeded nonchalantly to wash first his forepaws and then his whiskers and then behind his ears. The Queen was delighted and tentatively stretched out her hand towards Tomkin. As she touched the soft fur at the back of his head Tomkin gently rubbed against her hand, cameled his back, and began to purr.

'This is a complete cat!' announced the King. 'I will give you ten times the value of all the trade that we have already carried out in exchange for this extraordinary beast.'

The deal was struck, and the next morning the Unicorn set off back to England, to sail up the Thames and moor at the East India docks.

Tomkin moved into the kitchen of the King of Barbary's palace by day; he spent his evenings in the Banqueting Hall; and every night he slept in the Number One Queen's state bedroom, where he went seven times round before he settled to sleep. He became the most famous animal in all of Barbary, and later the King sent his royal messengers far and wide to find Tomkin a Queen. But that is another story.

Just below the village of Highgate, Dick stopped to rest beside the track and to eat the apples that he had picked up in the orchards in Islington. It was a clear day and he could see the massive spire of St Paul's and the lesser towers and spires of the other churches in the City of London far below him.

It was Sunday morning and all the church bells began to ring to call people to morning service. The sound of the bells was carried on a gentle autumn zephyr bearing the scent of the orchards on its breath.

Dick sighed. He missed his family, and yet what future was there in Pauntley? The City lay like a mirage below him. It had so shocked and disappointed him, and yet it held the key to all his dreams.

He closed his eyes and the bells seem to speak to him:

'Turn again, Whittington, Lord Mayor of London! Turn again, Whittington, thrice Mayor of London!' they said, over and over and over again.

He was woken by spots of rain on his face. 'I must go', he thought, 'before I get wet.' He stood and, without a moment's hesitation, set off purposefully back the way he had come, back to the City of London.

When Dick got back to Mr Fitzwarren's house in Leadenhall Street he knocked on the back door and Cook let him in. She smiled cheerfully for the first time since Dick had known her. 'Ha! Dick. You've missed your chance by skulking off like that. The Unicorn has docked, and we all had more for our things than we ever thought possible. You'd better get back to keeling your greasy pots!'

Alice was sitting sadly on the balcony. She had been very upset when they discovered Dick had left, without saying goodbye. She had such news for him, but no way to find him. Now she looked into the courtyard – and there he was!

She raced to the kitchen, flashed him a huge smile, grabbed him by the hand and positively hauled him upstairs.

'You have to come and see Papa!' she cried.

'But no, I'm – I can't – I'm just a scullery boy and I'm all dirty... and I left... and I didn't even thank him!'

Alice stamped her foot and said, 'Well, you can come now! It's the least you can do.' And then she giggled mischievously.

Mr Fitzwarren's eyes twinkled when he saw Dick, and he went up and down on his toes thoughtfully. 'Ah. Dick. Glad you're back. Hmm. Quirk of timing, I'd say. Yes. Quite. Hmm.'

'Oh, come on, Papa, tell him!' said Alice.

And then Dick heard about Tomkin at the feast and the rats, and that he was now living a pampered life as a hero in the Palace of the King of Barbary.

When Dick was told the price Tomkin had fetched, he felt dizzy and had to sit down, and then he leapt up, apologising for putting his grubby bottom on the cushions, and then he burst into tears. He asked Mr Fitzwarren to take most of the money, as he felt it was not really for him, but Mr Fitzwarren refused. 'You parted with your only possession, which you both loved and needed. All the money is yours.'

So Dick gave presents to all the other servants, including Cook, who smiled at Dick for the second time ever. Then he went to the public baths and got very, very clean, and then he had a haircut, and then he bought himself some smart new clothes and boots. He also bought a little golden brooch in the shape of a cat for Alice. He was surprised and baffled when her eyes seemed to brim with tears and her lower lip to tremble as she thanked him for it. Mr Fitzwarren noticed that too, and it set him thinking again.

And that is almost the happy ending of the story of Dick Whittington and his cat.

Dick married Alice Fitzwarren and they were terrifically happy, though they had no children. But they did have Big Puss, who lived to be 35 and spent all his time in bed, and after that they had Tomkin the Second and the Third, and many many more. And they sent two kittens to the Canons at St Frideswide's, which duly and daily served them.

The rest, as they say, is history. Real history. True history.

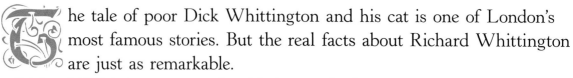

The tale of poor Dick Whittington and his cat is one of London's most famous stories. But the real facts about Richard Whittington are just as remarkable.

Richard Whittington was the third son of a landowner in Pauntley, who had been outlawed for marrying without the King's permission. Not being likely to inherit anything, he walked to London and was apprenticed to the Mercers. He built up his business as a trader importing fine silks and velvets and exporting wool and broadcloth. At first he worked with Mr Fitzwarren, and then created his own business. He became a Liveryman and later Master of the Mercers' Company, and even sold cloth to King Richard II for his Great Wardrobe. In 1402 he married Alice Fitzwarren.

Richard Whittington became Lord Mayor of the City of London in 1397.
He became Lord Mayor again in 1406…
And again in 1419!
He became very wealthy through trading and so he frequently lent money
to important people. He lent large sums to King Henry IV, who found it
very useful, and later King Henry V, where it helped with the Battle of
Agincourt in 1415. He also spent lots of his own money making things better
for other people.

He was a great philanthropist. He was so generous that he often did not ask for the debts to be paid back, even by the King! He tried very hard to spend his money making London a healthier, happier place for everybody.

He built the first public lavatories in London at St Martin Vintry, flushed by the high tide in the river Thames.

He funded the library at Greyfriars.

He rebuilt the Guildhall in the City of London.

He paid for drainage systems at Cripplegate and at Billingsgate.

Despite being a moneylender himself, he was so trusted and revered that he sat as a Judge on an important usury trial.

When he died, as he had no children, he left all his money to charity, to be looked after by the Worshipful Company of Mercers. This was used to rebuild Newgate prison and to add new facilities at St Bartholomew's Hospital. It also funded public drinking fountains and almshouses for the poor.

Even now, Dick Whittington's money is still funding many of the charitable activities of the Mercers' Company.

And you can find his statue, with Tomkin,
standing outside the Guildhall to this very day.

Clare Gifford has over recent years become greatly interested and involved in the life, history and culture of 'the City that made the world'. Her husband Roger was elected Lord Mayor of London for 2012–13.

She is also, as Dr. Taylor, a physician and pathologist who has worked for many years as a hospital consultant and with the UK blood services.

Clare has two children and lives in Camden Town and Scotland. This is her first children's book.

Emmanuel Cerisier was born in Rennes, France in 1970. After art school, he moved to Paris to work as an illustrator in children's publishing.

He specializes in illustrating non-fiction books, working in gouache. Emmanuel now lives with his family in Brittany.

Some characteristics of Tomkin were inspired
by descriptions of *Jeoffry* in the poem *Jubilate
Agno* by Chistopher Smart, written circa 1760.